# Beverly Lewis

# Beverly Lewis Books for Young Readers

## PICTURE BOOKS

*Annika's Secret Wish* • *Cows in the House*
*In Jesse's Shoes* • *Just Like Mama*
*What Is Heaven Like?*

## THE CUL-DE-SAC KIDS

*The Double Dabble Surprise*
*The Chicken Pox Panic*
*The Crazy Christmas Angel Mystery*
*No Grown-ups Allowed*
*Frog Power*
*The Mystery of Case D. Luc*
*The Stinky Sneakers Mystery*
*Pickle Pizza*
*Mailbox Mania*
*The Mudhole Mystery*
*Fiddlesticks*
*The Crabby Cat Caper*
*Tarantula Toes*
*Green Gravy*
*Backyard Bandit Mystery*
*Tree House Trouble*
*The Creepy Sleep-Over*
*The Great TV Turn-Off*
*Piggy Party*
*The Granny Game*
*Mystery Mutt*
*Big Bad Beans*
*The Upside-Down Day*
*The Midnight Mystery*

*Katie and Jake and the Haircut Mistake*

*www.BeverlyLewis.com*

THE CUL-DE-SAC KIDS

The Crabby
Cat Caper

Beverly Lewis

BETHANY HOUSE PUBLISHERS
MINNEAPOLIS, MINNESOTA 55438

*The Crabby Cat Caper*
Copyright © 1997
Beverly Lewis

Cover illustration by Paul Turnbaugh
Story illustrations by Janet Huntington

Published by Bethany House Publishers
11400 Hampshire Avenue South
Bloomington, Minnesota 55438

Bethany House Publishers is a division of
Baker Publishing Group, Grand Rapids, Michigan.

Printed in the United States of America

ISBN-13: 978-1-55661-912-0
ISBN-10: 1-55661-912-X

**Library of Congress Cataloging-in-Publication Data**

Lewis, Beverly, 1949–
    The crabby cat caper / Beverly Lewis.
      p.   cm. — (The cul-de-sac kids ; #12)
    Summary: Dee Dee looks forward to showing her cat
Mister Whiskers in the pet parade at the school carnival, but
then he disappears before she can get him to school.
    ISBN 1-55661-912-X
    [1. Cats—Fiction. 2. Pet shows—Fiction. 3. Pets—
Fiction.] I. Title. II. Series: Lewis, Beverly, 1949–
Cul-de-sac kids ; 12.
PZ7.L58464Co     1996
[Fic]—dc21                      96–45851
                                 CIP
                                 AC

For Janet Huntington,
who draws the pictures
in these books
and
who lives with
two very crabby cats—
Nancy and Little John.

THE CUL-DE-SAC KIDS

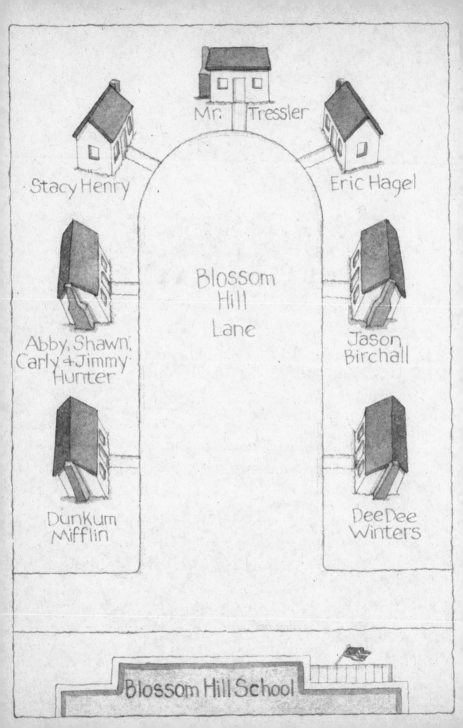

# ONE

"Yucko," said Dee Dee Winters. "Thinking up riddles is hard."

She stared out her bedroom window. She tapped her pencil on the desk.

It was almost summer. The last day of May.

Two weeks till summer vacation.

Two days till the school carnival.

*Meow*. Mister Whiskers curled against Dee Dee's legs.

"I have to write a riddle for school," she told him. "Any ideas?"

*Merrrt.* Mister Whiskers shook his furry body. His name tag jingled.

"Don't tell me no," Dee Dee said. "You haven't even tried."

Mister Whiskers found a sunny spot on the floor. He licked his sleek, gray coat.

His whiskers wiggled. They waggled.

*Purrr.* The sound was like a motor boat. A soft, distant one.

"Is that all you have to say?" Dee Dee rolled her dark eyes. "You're no help."

Mister Whiskers stretched his soft body against the carpet.

"So . . . just like that, you're takin' a nap?" Dee Dee said.

The long whiskers twitched. Dreamland was on its way.

*What can I expect?* she thought. *He's a cat. A crabby little cat.*

She was right. Mister Whiskers was definitely crabby. Sometimes worse than crabby. Sometimes he took risks.

Big ones!

Daring thrills and certain chills.
Potted plant spills from windowsills.
Sometimes he set off fire drills.
That's what Mister Whiskers was all about.

Dee Dee picked up her pencil. She decided to try to write the riddle again.

"Everyone in class has to write one," Dee Dee explained to her sleepy cat. "The riddle is due Monday."

She checked her kitty calendar. The May border had cat paws along the side.

"This is Friday afternoon," Dee Dee said. "I better hurry."

*Mew.* Mister Whiskers opened one droopy eye.

"You agree with me? Well, it's about time." Dee Dee laughed.

She picked up her pencil. She wrote:

*A Riddle*
*by*
*Dee Dee Winters*

12

She stopped. "Now what? What comes next?"

Mister Whiskers didn't open his eyes this time. The cozy cat was somewhere in snooze land. Probably dreaming about his supper. Or his next adventure.

Dee Dee made kissy noises. She did it three times.

No response.

"Fine and dandy," she whispered. "Sleep your life away."

But Dee Dee didn't want Mister Whiskers to sleep. Not at all. She wanted his eyes wide open. She wanted his tail jerking.

Dee Dee wanted company. Someone to talk to. Even if it was only cat chat!

# TWO

Dee Dee started to write again. But her pencil was dull. She went to her pencil sharpener. All the while, she was thinking about her riddle.

"I've got it!" she said at last. "I know what I'll write!" Dee Dee hurried to her desk.

Neatly, she printed these words:

> *I am green.*
> *I make a certain cat hiss.*
> *I have blinky eyes and eat flies.*
> *Who am I?*
> *Hint: My name starts with C.*

She put her pencil down and read the riddle and the hint. She thought about it.

Then she read it again. This time out loud.

Dee Dee wasn't sure if she liked it. "Everyone will know the answer," she said. "It's too easy."

She thought about Jason Birchall's frog, Croaker. The bullfrog made her cat go crazy. Totally goofy.

The Cul-de-sac Kids were going to take pets to the school carnival. They wanted to walk around and show them off.

Yesterday, they'd had a big meeting about it. A Cul-de-sac Kids meeting. All pet decisions had been made.

Stacy Henry was taking Sunday Funnies, her white cockapoo. Dunkum Mifflin was putting a leash on his rabbit, Blinkee.

Eric Hagel was taking Fran the Ham, his girl hamster. He would carry her around in his shirt pocket.

Shawn Hunter was taking Snow White, his floppy-eared puppy. Carly and Jimmy Hunter wanted to take their pet ducks, Quacker and Jack.

*Ducks at a carnival?* thought Dee Dee.

She had nearly burst out laughing. How could that possibly work? But she'd kept quiet at the meeting.

And there was Croaker to think about.

She'd asked Jason to keep his bullfrog home. "Don't frogs need to be in water?"

At first, Jason argued. "You're just saying that because you don't want Mister Whiskers to have a hissy fit."

"You're right," she said. "So *please* keep your frog at home!"

Jason had pouted.

But Dee Dee won him over. "I'll make some cookies."

"My favorite?" Jason asked.

Jason wasn't supposed to eat chocolate. It wound him up. But carob

17

chip cookies tasted a lot like chocolate chip cookies.

"I'll bring them to school on Monday," Dee Dee said.

So it was settled.

Mister Whiskers could attend the carnival *purr*fectly happy. And Croaker would stay home in his aquarium.

*Where he belongs*, thought Dee Dee.

She stood up and looked out the window. From her bedroom, she could see Blossom Hill School. Jason's father and some other men were working. They were building the booths for the carnival.

"I can't wait till Monday," Dee Dee said. "The carnival will be so much fun!"

She turned to look at her cat.

But Mister Whiskers was gone.

"Where'd you go?" Dee Dee said.

She searched under her bed. It was Mister Whiskers' favorite hiding spot. "Here kitty, kitty," she called.

No cat.

She ran downstairs to the kitchen. *Maybe he's hungry*, she thought.

But Mister Whiskers wasn't eating from his dish. He wasn't drinking milk from his bowl, either.

"Where *are* you?" she cried.

She checked under the telephone table. Sometimes he sat on the phone book.

Today, he wasn't there.

She searched all the windowsills. Mostly the ones with potted plants.

No Mister Whiskers.

*Where could he be?* she thought.

Then she had an idea.

Maybe he'd gotten out. He liked to run loose in the cul-de-sac. He was always running away.

The back screen door hung open sometimes. It had to be tugged hard to give it a snug fit.

Eagerly, Dee Dee checked the front and back doors. They were shut tight.

There was no way for Mister Whiskers to escape. Not today.

Dee Dee was stumped. Her cat had tricked her.

"You'll be sorry!" she hollered up the steps. "You won't get your afternoon cookie."

She sat down on the living room floor.

Under her breath, she counted. "One . . . two . . . three . . . four . . ."

Before she got to five, Mister Whiskers came. He padded down the steps, looking shy. A little uneasy, too.

Dee Dee saw bits of paper around his mouth. "What have you been doing?" she said.

*Meow*. Mister Whiskers stared at her with his sly yellow-orange eyes. Slowly, he blinked.

"Come here, you!" She picked the pieces out of his whiskers.

Finally, all the bits of paper were in the trash.

21

Dee Dee remembered the way her cat had blinked at her. Something else had eyes like that. Well, sort of.

Croaker, Jason's bullfrog, had tricky eyes, too.

"You stay right here." Dee Dee wagged her finger in his furry face. "Don't you dare move!"

She ran upstairs. She ran so fast, her hair bow fell off.

Dee Dee was determined. She was going to find out what trouble Mister Whiskers was up to.

Right now!

# THREE

Dee Dee scurried to her bedroom. Slowly she scanned the room with her eyes.

Then she spotted it. Plain as day.

There, on the floor, were pieces of shredded paper. Right beside her desk.

"Why, that little crab cake!" Dee Dee muttered. "He tore up my riddle."

Then she remembered. The riddle was about Croaker. She'd read it out loud.

But she thought Mister Whiskers hadn't heard it. She thought he was sound asleep.

*He tricked me again,* she thought.

Dee Dee dashed downstairs. "You really don't like that bullfrog, do you?" she said.

*Merrrt.* The furry face replied. It was cat chat for "nope."

"Well, I don't blame you," Dee Dee said. "But that doesn't mean you can rip up my riddle."

Mister Whiskers slinked down. Like he was going to pounce on a mouse.

"OK, that does it," Dee Dee said. "Crabby cats don't sleep in *my* room. Downstairs—to the cellar!"

*Meoorsy?*

"That's right, the cellar," she insisted.

Mister Whiskers hated the cellar. It was dark, musty, and lonely.

No people.

No soft beds.

No canned tuna!

Mister Whiskers' face suddenly changed. No more sly look. Not the

24

uneasy-looking one, either. The kind that said: *I'm in trouble!*

Now the kitty mouth was turned down. The eyelids drooped to narrow slits. A very sour look ruled his face.

Dee Dee tore into him. "What a crab cake you are! Why don't you behave yourself?"

He whined and spit like he'd been kicked.

Dee Dee said, "You must learn a hard lesson."

She leaned over to pick him up.

*Whoosh!* Mister Whiskers flew out of her reach.

"Hey!" she shouted. "Come back here!"

Dee Dee chased her cat around the living room.

Mister Whiskers darted into the dining room. And sailed under the table. He weaved through the maze of chair legs. Always, just out of her reach.

"Mister Whiskers!" she squealed. "Stop!"

But it was no use. Her cat was angry.

Cellars were for dogs. And garbage cans.

Cats deserved far better.

Dee Dee was almost certain those were Mister Whiskers' kitty thoughts.

Out of breath, she stopped trailing him. She sat down on one of the dining room chairs.

A great idea popped into her head, and she began to smile.

"Wanna bake some cookies?" she called. "Here kitty, kitty . . . cookie." That would surely bring him running.

Fast as a mouse, Mister Whiskers jumped up on her lap. He licked his chops. He looked so cute—eyes all perky. Tail all swishy.

As she stared at him, Dee Dee felt sorry. Her great idea fell flat. She couldn't banish Mister Whiskers to the cellar.

Not now. Not later.

"Aw, you silly crab cake," she said. And Dee Dee kissed his soft, little head.

*Meoorry.*

"I know you're sorry," she said. "Now, let's bake Jason's cookies. He'll keep his frog home from the carnival if we do." She grinned at her cat. "Then *you* can go with me."

Mister Whiskers seemed pleased. He puffed out his body and nuzzled Dee Dee's face.

"Wanna help?"

She didn't have to ask twice. Dee Dee knew her cat well. Very well.

# FOUR

After supper, Mrs. Winters served dessert.

Dee Dee carried in a bowl of peaches. Next came some whipped cream—the real stuff.

"Yummers!" she said.

Mister Whiskers was perched on the floor beside her chair. His eyes were on the sweet whipped cream.

"I made carob chip cookies today," Dee Dee announced. "My cat and I did."

Her father's eyes danced. "Sounds delicious."

Dee Dee set a plateful of cookies on the kitchen table. "We made extra," she said.

Her mother smiled. "You must've cooked up something with your cul-de-sac friends."

Dee Dee nodded. "Jason wanted to take his frog to the school carnival. But if he did, then I couldn't take Mister Whiskers."

Her father looked up. "Why not?"

"Because my cat hates that frog," she said.

"Well, seems to me your cat pretty much runs things around here," her father said.

"I know," Dee Dee said. "But he's so cute and cuddly—that's why."

But she knew differently. Mister Whiskers was a cranky, crabby cat. That's why he got his way. Most of the time.

"Anyway, we made the cookies for Jason," Dee Dee explained. "He won't mind leaving his frog home."

Her parents traded glances.

Dee Dee noticed. "Well, I *am* being nice to Jason," she said. "Not mean like Mister Whiskers is sometimes."

"Not just sometimes," her father said. "That cat is a real pain *most* of the time."

Dee Dee reached down and tickled Mister Whiskers' neck. She hoped he hadn't heard.

★   ★   ★

After supper, Dee Dee played with her cat. She scratched his left ear. Mister Whiskers liked it there best.

"You did a good job today," she said. "You licked the cookie bowl nice and clean."

*Meoow-mew*.

"You're welcome," Dee Dee said. "Now I have to write my riddle for school."

She carried the cat upstairs. "Promise not to eat my homework this time?"

Mister Whiskers was quiet.

31

"Oh, you're not making any promises, is that it?" Dee Dee sighed. She frisked Mister Whiskers' chin.

"To be truthful, I didn't like the bull-frog riddle either," she told her cat.

Dee Dee picked up her pencil. She set to work.

Mister Whiskers helped, too. He helped by settling into a cozy spot. Right on Dee Dee's bed.

It sure beat the cellar. Any day!

# FIVE

The next day was Saturday.

Dee Dee's doorbell rang after break-fast.

Mister Whiskers was sunning himself. He liked to sit by the living room window.

When the doorbell rang, he sniffed the air. He could almost smell a bullfrog.

Dee Dee opened the door.

"Hi, Jason," she said.

Jason hopped around a bit. Then he said, "I came over for my cookies."

Dee Dee frowned. "That's not what we agreed on."

"I don't care," he said. "I can't wait till Monday. I want them *now*."

"Well, too bad." Dee Dee reached for the doorknob.

Jason stuck his foot in the door. "The deal's off. I'm taking Croaker to the carnival."

With that, he pulled his bullfrog out of his jacket.

Mister Whiskers spied the frog. In a flash, he leaped off his window perch.

*Hiss-ss! Phttt!* He was going goofy.

"Get your cat away!" Jason hollered. "I mean it!"

Just then Mrs. Winters came into the living room. "What on earth is going on?"

She saw Jason holding his bullfrog.

"Uh, Jason," she said, "would you mind stepping outside with that uh . . . uh . . ."

"This is Croaker." He held the bullfrog high.

Mrs. Winters waved her hands.

"Please take him outside!"

By now, Mister Whiskers was having a royal fit. He spread his long claws. He even tried to follow Jason and his bullfrog outside.

But Jason backed away. "I . . . I have to go help my dad now," he said. "'Bye, Dee Dee!"

With a great burst of speed, he rushed down the front steps.

Mister Whiskers pushed his nose against the screen door. Still fussing at Croaker.

Dee Dee caught him just in time. "Oh no you don't," she said. "You're not going near that frog!"

The cat's eyes squinted into a sly slant.

*Merrrt!* He leaped up onto his sunny sill.

Mister Whiskers sat tall. King of kitties.

With hope in his eyes, he watched Jason walk across the street. He saw him head for the school. He knew the bullfrog was in Jason's pocket.

The sun began to warm Mister Whiskers again. He relaxed, washing his paws in the sunlight.

Soon, he began to daydream. His kitty dream was filled with sweet freedom. He could almost taste the green grass. A young, juicy field mouse . . .

*Purrr.* Mister Whiskers snoozed. Running away was his best dream yet.

The hot sun poured through the bay window.

He was bigger than a mountain lion. He could outrun anything. Mice and dogs. Even a bullfrog!

Only inches to go. He was that close to catching the ugly green frog. . . .

★  ★  ★

"Wake up, kitty," Dee Dee called.
She went to the windowsill. Gently,

37

she picked him up and carried him to the kitchen.

"Time for some din-din."

Her cat yawned and stretched.

"Oh, you poor thing. You're so tired," Dee Dee said. She put him down. He could hardly stand up.

Then she opened the fridge. "Cold milk will perk you up." She turned her back, still cooing to her cat.

But someone had forgotten to tug on the back screen door. It was hanging open a crack.

Just enough.

# SIX

Dee Dee stood in the middle of the kitchen. She couldn't believe her eyes.

"Mister Whiskers was right here!" she explained to her mother.

"He'll come back," Mrs. Winters said.

Dee Dee went to the back door and looked out. *He's a house cat*, she thought. *He needs to be indoors.*

She turned to her mother. "Mister Whiskers has always wanted his freedom," she said. "I can tell by the look in his eyes."

She sniffled.

Mrs. Winters slipped her arm around Dee Dee. "Don't worry, honey."

But Dee Dee *was* worried. She was very worried.

What if Mister Whiskers didn't want to come home?

What then?

★ ★ ★

Later, Dee Dee helped her father sweep the porch.

"I don't want to wait for Mister Whiskers to come home," she said. "I want to go find him."

Mr. Winters nodded with a grunt. Then he went to get the garden hose.

"I'm gonna look for him," Dee Dee said. "As soon as I'm finished here."

"OK with me," Mr. Winters mumbled. He began to hose down the front porch.

Dee Dee knew her dad wasn't very worried. Maybe he was secretly glad.

"Do you miss our cat?" she asked.

"Miss who?" he said. "*Our* cat?"

"Well, you know," Dee Dee said softly.

She wished her dad thought of Mister Whiskers that way. She wished he thought of the cat as family.

At last, Dee Dee's chores were done. She set off down the cul-de-sac.

First, she stopped at Jason Birchall's house next door.

"My cat ran off," she told Jason's mother.

"I'm sorry to hear that," Mrs. Birchall said. "I'll tell Jason to watch for him."

"Thanks," said Dee Dee.

She went to Eric Hagel's house. He lived in the house next to Jason. Eric's grandpa was sitting on the porch.

"Have you seen my cat?" Dee Dee asked.

Grandpa Hagel yawned. "Can't say that I have."

"If you see him, will you let me know?" she asked.

The old man nodded. "I'd be glad to."

Mr. Tressler lived at the very end of Blossom Hill Lane. Dee Dee headed there next.

She rang the doorbell.

Seconds passed, and Mr. Tressler opened the door. "Hello there, little missy," he said. "What can I do for you?"

"Just thought you'd seen my cat."

Mr. Tressler leaned on his cane. "Run off, eh?"

Dee Dee nodded. "I think he wants his freedom."

"Could be," he said. "But a well-fed pet always returns."

"Really?" she said. This was good news.

"Yes, indeedy." Mr. Tressler jiggled his cane.

"So . . . Mister Whiskers will come home!" She scampered down the opposite side of the cul-de-sac. It was Stacy Henry's side of the street.

She turned to go toward Stacy's house. But stopped. "Wait a minute," she said out loud. "A well-fed pet always comes home. Mr. Tressler said so."

So she decided not to bother looking. Her cat could come dragging home when he was ready. Probably around supper-time.

*I'll go help at the carnival*, she thought.

And that's what she did.

★ ★ ★

Much later, Dee Dee poured milk into Mister Whiskers' bowl. She set it outside near the back door.

"This'll bring him back," she said.

Her mother agreed. "Good idea."

Dee Dee waited and watched. She waited some more.

She waited till supper.

No cat.

She waited till *after* supper.

No Mister Whiskers.

She waited till bedtime.

Nothing.

She tiptoed downstairs after her mother had tucked her in.

Still no sign of her cat.

Dee Dee unhooked the back screen door. She let it hang open. Just enough.

She sat on the floor, waiting. She waited till the moon slid over Jason's roof next door.

But Mister Whiskers didn't come home.

*That crab cake!* thought Dee Dee.

# SEVEN

Dee Dee got up early Sunday morning. She dashed downstairs.

The screen door was locked now. She unlatched it and went outside.

She checked the kitty bowl. Sour milk. "Yuk!" She dumped it out.

Back inside, she woke up her parents. "Mister Whiskers didn't come home," Dee Dee told them.

Her father rolled over. He made husky, early-morning sounds under the covers.

Her mother sat up. She stroked Dee

Dee's hair. "Oh, he'll come home. You'll see."

Dee Dee kept watch for her cat. Even after breakfast. And between teeth-brushing and getting ready for church.

Soon, it was time to leave for Sunday school.

During prayer time, Dee Dee talked to God. "Please take care of my cat," she whispered.

★ ★ ★

After dinner, Dee Dee went to see Carly Hunter. She and Carly were best friends.

She told Carly about her runaway cat. "I hope he comes back real soon," she said sadly.

"Me too," Carly said. "It would be lonely at your house without him."

Dee Dee sighed. "My dad doesn't think so. He'd probably care more if we got a dog."

Carly giggled. "How can you say that?"

"Some people like dogs best," Dee Dee replied. "I think my dad's a dog person."

Carly played with her long curls. "Dogs aren't better than cats." She turned to look at Dee Dee. "Did you ask God to help you find him?"

Dee Dee nodded. "At church."

"Then don't worry," Carly suggested.

Dee Dee smiled. "OK, I'll try not to."

And she did try.

She tried so hard, she almost forgot about Mister Whiskers.

On Monday, she gave Jason his cookies. At lunch, the kids talked about the carnival. Jason was busy eating his carob chip cookies.

After recess, Dee Dee turned in her riddle. It went like this:

*A Riddle*
*by*
*Dee Dee Winters*

*I help bake cookies.*
*And eat them, too.*

*Sometimes I act like a crab cake.*
*I speak a secret language.*
*And I love freedom!*
*Who am I?*
*Clue: none.*

Dee Dee didn't bother telling Jason that her cat was still missing.

After school, the Cul-de-sac Kids met at Abby's house.

Abby Hunter was the president of the club. "We don't have to have another meeting, do we?" she asked.

No one wanted another meeting. They were too excited about the carnival.

"Double dabble good," Abby said. "No meeting. Let's go!"

They made a circle and locked hands. "Cul-de-sac Kids stick together," they chanted.

At the end of their block, they crossed the street together. Kids and pets.

Abby Hunter was the only one without

a pet. Dee Dee Winters had one, but it was absent—a runaway.

Jason Birchall chomped on his cookies—the perfect reward for leaving his frog behind. Only now, with Mister Whiskers gone, he could've brought Croaker along, Dee Dee thought.

But she decided not to say anything. Jason would probably figure it out.

Soon, the Cul-de-sac Kids were exploring the carnival. They showed off their pets.

"It's a pet parade," Jason said to Dee Dee. "Remember the one we had last Easter?"

Dee Dee remembered.

Suddenly, Jason's eyes grew big. "Hey!" he shouted.

"What's wrong?" Dee Dee asked.

"Your cat's not here," he said. "So why can't Croaker come to the carnival?"

Dee Dee couldn't think of a reason. Well, she could. But she didn't want to cause trouble. Not now. Not here at the carnival.

"I wanna show off my pet!" Jason said.

"Then go home and get him," Dee Dee replied.

And with that, Jason left the school grounds. He ran all the way home.

Dee Dee hoped he was doing the right thing. What if the other pets starting hissing at Croaker?

But she knew she didn't have to worry. Dogs and ducks couldn't care less about bullfrogs. Neither did rabbits and hamsters.

*Cats* were the ones who hissed and spit. They had hissy fits. At least, Mister Whiskers always did.

But today, Dee Dee wouldn't have to worry about her crabby cat. Mister Whiskers was gone. Having a long taste of freedom.

He was far away from home by now.

Maybe many miles away.

# EIGHT

The House of Mirrors was a frightful place. A scaredy-cat place.

Mister Whiskers opened one eye. Bravely, he took another peek. He was big as a mountain lion. This was not a dream!

He stared at the strange mirror. Both eyes wide. That face . . . and those ears. Had he always looked this way?

Suddenly, he heard voices. A familiar voice stood out. It was Dee Dee's, his favorite girl-person.

*Merrrt!* Mister Whiskers couldn't let

her find him. Not now. Not yet!

There were too many wonderful smells and sounds. He was enjoying freedom. And people food!

Since running away, he'd begun to understand life on the outside. Now he knew why humans ate junk food.

*Mm-m-meoowsy!* Scraps of French fries and bits of hot dog. And melted ice cream on wrappers.

Mister Whiskers loved his new life!

But he hid when Dee Dee and her friends came near. He slinked away, out of sight. He crawled behind the tallest mirror.

Dee Dee and Carly posed in front of the fat mirror. They were giggling and talking.

"Let's tell Jason to bring Croaker in here," Carly said.

Dee Dee grinned. "That bullfrog will look fatter than ever!"

The girls tried out the tall, skinny

mirror. And all the others.

When they left, they were still laughing.

Mister Whiskers felt something tickle his insides. A homesick bug, maybe?

Or was it the junk food?

Suddenly a familiar scent hit his nose. He sniffed the air.

The muscles in his furry body froze. The hair on his back stood in a ridge.

He sniffed again. What was that horrid smell?

Then he knew. His claws shot out. *FROG!*

Mister Whiskers crept close to the ground. He slinked under the tall mirror. He wanted to find that bullfrog.

He *had* to find him!

Mister Whiskers peeked out from under the tall mirror. He spied himself—a very fat self—a few feet away—in the fat mirror.

Jason was holding his bullfrog in front

of the fat mirror, too.

*Rribbittt!* Croaker spotted Mister Whiskers! The bullfrog leaped out of Jason's hands.

"What?" Jason said, spinning around.

*Boink—boink!* The frog hopped out of the House of Mirrors. He headed for the dunk tank.

The principal was sitting in the dunking chair. He sat high above the water.

*Wheeee!* Croaker leaped up and flew over the fence. He splashed down, into the water tank.

Mister Whiskers was close behind. He tried to make the fence.

*Splaaat!* Not quite.

He fell to the ground, staring at the fence. He hissed at his poor judgment.

Then he heard a sound. *Quack, quack-ity-quack!*

Cracker and Jack were loose. They were waddling toward him. Their thin rope leashes dragged behind.

*Merrrt!* Mister Whiskers didn't like the looks of those long beaks. He arched his back.

But nope, it wasn't worth a fit. Those slow-pokey ducks would never catch him. Nothing to hiss about.

He turned his attention back to the bullfrog.

Croaker was swimming around having a good time. Safe inside the dunk tank!

Mister Whiskers stared at him. Could *he* swim today? Should he risk one of his nine lives?

Suddenly, out of the corner of his eye, he saw a fluff of white. Snow White, Shawn's dog, was charging at him!

*Zoom!* Mister Whiskers darted away from the dunk tank. He zipped toward the food stand, under the popcorn maker. Past the hot dogs and around two trash cans.

Snow White was on his tail. She was

58

panting just inches away. He felt the slobber on his hind legs.

Mister Whiskers was in big trouble. He kept moving.

Faster . . . faster!

# NINE

*Arfff!* Stacy's cockapoo joined the chase. Behind him, two rabbit ears flopped in the air. Dunkum waved his empty dog leash, trying to catch Blinkee.

*Meoorsy?* Mister Whiskers longed for the cellar at home. So what if it was dark and musty? It was safe!

Just then he heard his girl-person. "Kitty, kitty . . . cookie!" she called.

He glanced behind him. One split second.

*Merrrt!* No way would he fall for the cookie trick.

A whole trail of things was coming after him. And he was *purr*ty sure there was no cookie.

Maybe someday he'd have time for a real cookie. If he lived to tell the story.

★　★　★

Dee Dee grabbed Carly's hand. "Quick! Help me catch my cat!"

Carly scrambled along after Dee Dee.

They chased the pets through the maze of carnival booths. Two ducks, two dogs, one rabbit, and a crabby cat.

The one and only frog caught the action from a slippery perch. He'd come up for air, next to the principal's dunking chair. The kids were pointing and yelling.

Fran the Ham watched the chase, too. She was safe and dry in Eric's pocket.

Dee Dee and Carly dashed past the ducks. The girls were gaining on Sunday Funnies now.

Then Dee Dee heard it . . .

*Meoowp!* Mister Whiskers was crying for help.

She could see him leading the chase. He was headed for the kiddie rides.

Dee Dee sped up. "Hurry, Carly!"

But Carly was out of breath. "I can't run any faster."

Dee Dee lost sight of Mister Whiskers. She stopped running. "We'll never catch him now," she gasped. "Not in all those rides."

The girls peered into the distance. Dee Dee spied Quacker and Jack. They were the last animals into the rides area.

"Come on," Dee Dee said. "We have to get Abby and the others to help us. Our pets could get hurt in there."

Carly followed her back through a tangle of booths and stands.

At last, they found Abby and Stacy. And the other Cul-de-sac Kids. All of them had been searching in the wrong places.

"The pets are over there," Dee Dee

shouted. She pointed toward the busy kiddie rides.

Abby said, "That could be dangerous."

Dee Dee frowned. "What'll we do?"

"Round up all the Cul-de-sac Kids,"
she said. "If we stick together, we can
catch our pets."

Dee Dee smiled. Abby always talked
about sticking together as friends. Maybe
that's why she was president of their club.

All nine kids hurried toward the
amusement area. There were lots of rides.
Even a Ferris wheel.

Dee Dee and Carly passed through the
kiddie ride gate.

High overhead, the Ferris wheel rose
like a tower.

Dee Dee looked up . . . up. Up!

She cupped her hand over her eyes.
Then she saw something.

Could it be?

It was!

"Abby, look!" she cried. "My cat's riding on the Ferris wheel!"

The Cul-de-sac Kids gasped. They stared up at Mister Whiskers.

"He's up there, all right," Jason said. "And I bet he ate my frog!"

Dee Dee was worried. Mister Whiskers *did* look a bit green.

Then someone in the crowd called out, "There's a frog at the dunk tank. He's with the principal."

"Thanks!" Jason said. He ran off to get Croaker.

Dee Dee sighed. Thank goodness! Her cat had behaved himself. He had *not* gobbled down Jason's frog!

Then . . .

*Screeeech!* There was a horrible, loud scraping sound.

*Bam!* The Ferris wheel came to a grinding stop.

"Oh no!" shouted Dee Dee. "Look!"

The kids saw where she was pointing. More gulps came from the crowd.

"The Ferris wheel is stuck," Dee Dee hollered. "My cat's on the highest seat!"

And he was. The poor little cat dangled in midair. He stood up and leaned out over the side. He looked down at his girl-person.

*Meooooooowp!*

"We'll help you, kitty!" Dee Dee called to him. "Just don't jump! Please, Mister Whiskers, don't jump!"

But he didn't seem to hear the warning.

Mister Whiskers, eager for freedom, strained his neck. He reached out and pawed the air.

On the ground far below, Dee Dee shook with fear.

Her cul-de-sac friends shouted up to the cat, "Don't jump!"

Dee Dee closed her eyes. She couldn't watch.

She squeezed her eyes tight. "Please, God, don't let Mister Whiskers die."

# TEN

Mister Whiskers stared down. Down at the ground.

The hair on his back stuck straight out.

He heard his girl-person calling. She was saying something about having cookies later. Cookies and milk.

Her cheerful voice comforted him. So did the cookie word. Trick or not.

Mister Whiskers pulled his paw back in. He tried to forget about freedom. Bungee jumping without a cord was dumb.

He sat tall. King of kitties.

Then he heard a loud wail.

What was that?

He licked his paws. The paws that had almost nabbed that frog. Almost!

By the way, where *was* Croaker?

From his high perch, Mister Whiskers looked out over the carnival grounds. He could see Croaker's boy-person. Jason, they called him.

Jason was at the dunking tank. So was that bullfrog.

Mister Whiskers felt much too excited. He stretched his neck to see better. He imagined the bullfrog in front of his nose. Right there in the air!

He swung a left power paw. Then jabbed a right. That frog was *hiss*story!

Then . . .

*Whoosh!*

Mister Whiskers lost his balance.

And . . .

*Wheeeee!*

70

He was flying.
No. He was falling.

Down
    down . . .
        he fell.

★   ★   ★

"Let's catch him!" yelled Dee Dee.

The Cul-de-sac Kids made their circle. They locked hands.

*Ker-plop!* Mister Whiskers landed in the middle.

"Cul-de-sac Kids stick together," the kids chanted.

Mister Whiskers was a bit dazed by the fall. But he seemed glad for the circle of soft, human hands.

Dee Dee hugged him. She covered his head with kitty kisses. "Oh, baby, you're safe," she said.

Just then the hook-and-ladder truck arrived.

Dee Dee carried her cat over to the fire chief. She explained what happened. "It's a happy ending," she said.

When the fire truck left, Dunkum went looking for the other pets. Stacy, Shawn, Carly, and Jimmy helped, too.

It didn't take long to find Snow White and Sunday Funnies. And Blinkee and the ducks. The merry-go-round stopped. The dizzy pets were rescued.

Dunkum laughed. "Did you ever see a bunch of animals on a kiddie ride?"

Jason jigged around. "They probably thought the horses were for real."

Dee Dee liked the joke.

*Mew.* Mister Whiskers liked it, too.

The crabby cat caper was over.

Dee Dee's cat lived to *meow* about it. To have cookies and milk at bedtime. And lots of extra kissy hugs.

★ ★ ★

The next day, Dee Dee's father stroked

Mister Whiskers. He called him, "our pretty kitty."

Dee Dee was glad. Mister Whiskers really *was* part of the family!

He'd learned his lesson. Maybe he'd behave himself from now on. Maybe he wouldn't be such a crab cake.

"Here kitty, kitty . . . cookie," Dee Dee called. She grinned.

The cookie trick worked.

*This* time.

# THE CUL-DE-SAC KIDS SERIES
## Don't miss #13!

# TARANTULA TOES

Jason Birchall is starting a zoo—in his bedroom! Besides a bullfrog, Jason now owns a tarantula. A big, hairy super spider!

And he knows a secret about his new pet. Something he refuses to tell even his friends in the cul-de-sac. Especially not Abby Hunter and the girls!

Will Jason use his scary-looking pet to trick money out of his best pals? Can he fool *everyone* on Blossom Hill Lane?

# ABOUT THE AUTHOR

Beverly Lewis loves cats! Goldie and Angie were her childhood kittens. They spoke "cat chat" the same way Mister Whiskers does in this book.

Here's the "cat chat" chart:

*Merrrt*—Nope, no way.

*Meow*—Yes (or just wants attention).

*Mew*—Sure thing, yep.

*Meoory*—Sorry.

*Meoow-mew*—Thank you.

*Meoowsy*—Wow!

*Mm-m-meowsy!*—Mm-m good, tasty.

*Meoowp!*—Help!

*Meoorsy* means cellar. But Beverly's cats never used that word. Dee Dee's cat must've made it up.

If you like humor and mystery, get all the books in the Cul-de-sac Kids series. But watch out—your pets might "ask" you to read to them!